SIMON SPOTLIGHT & NICKELODEON
PRESENT:

· EXTREME RESCUE ·

HAWK MISSION

ERICA DAVID	WARNER MCGEE
writer	artist

NICK SCIACCA	KARA SARGENT	ALISON VELEA
designer	editor	managing editor

SIMON SPOTLIGHT/NICKELODEON   NEW YORK   LONDON   TORONTO   SYDNEY

BASED ON THE TV SERIES *GO, DIEGO, GO!*™ AS SEEN ON NICK JR.®

SIMON SPOTLIGHT
AN IMPRINT OF SIMON & SCHUSTER CHILDREN'S PUBLISHING DIVISION
1230 AVENUE OF THE AMERICAS, NEW YORK, NEW YORK 10020
FIRST EDITION 10 9 8 7 6 5 4 3 2 1
ISBN-13: 978-1-4169-7228-0   ISBN-10: 1-4169-7228-5

IF BABY HAWK DOESN'T KNOW HOW TO FLY YET, HE PROBABLY WALKED OFF . . . WHICH MEANS HE PROBABLY LEFT TRACKS!

HERE THEY ARE!

DIEGO FOLLOWED THE TRACKS TO AN OPEN FIELD.

THE TRACKS STOP HERE, BUT THERE'S NO SIGN OF BABY HAWK!

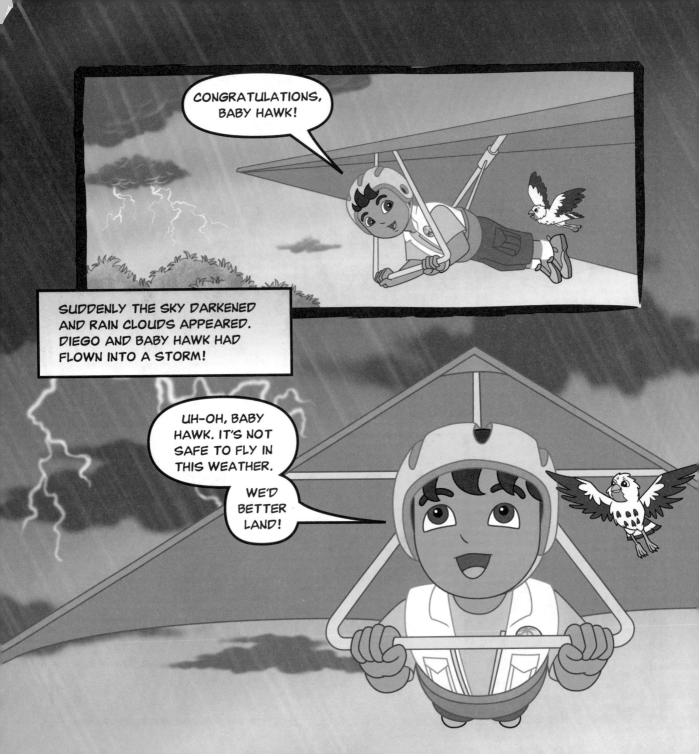

RESCUE PACK APPEARED AGAIN AND TURNED INTO A RAFT. DIEGO AND BABY HAWK CLIMBED ABOARD AND SET OUT TO CROSS THE RIVER.

BABY HAWK FLEW ALL THE WAY UP TO THE TOP OF THE TREE. DIEGO FOLLOWED BY CLIMBING UP THE TREE WITH A VINE.